YOKO & FRIENDS
SCHOOL DAYS

Doris's Dinosaur

Text and jacket art by
Rosemary Wells

Interior illustrations by
John Nez

Hyperion Books for Children
New York

Volo and the Volo colophon are trademarks of Disney Enterprises, Inc.
Hyperion Books for Children, 114 Fifth Avenue,
New York, New York 10011-5690.

Printed in the United States of America

First Edition
3 5 7 9 10 8 6 4 2

LIBRARY OF CONGRESS CATALOGING-IN-PUBLICATION DATA

Wells, Rosemary.
Doris's dinosaur / Rosemary Wells.—1st ed.
p.   cm.—(Yoko and friends—school days)
Summary: When Mrs. Jenkins proposes the class paint dinosaurs, Doris's unusual
artistic talent is not recognized until the class visits a modern art museum.
ISBN 0-7868-0726-1 (hardcover)—ISBN 0-7868-1532-9 (pbk.)
[1. Schools—Fiction. 2. Dinosaurs—Fiction. 3. Painting—Fiction.
4. Individuality—Fiction. 5. Beavers—Fiction. 6. Animals—Fiction.] I. Title.
PZ7.W46843 Do 2001
[E]—dc21   00—58161

Visit www.hyperionchildrensbooks.com

"What are we studying,

boys and girls?"

asked Mrs. Jenkins.

"Dinosaurs!" answered everybody.

"Yes!" said Mrs. Jenkins.

"Now it is time to decorate

the halls of Hilltop School

with our paintings of dinosaurs.

"Try and paint the best dinosaur
you can. You may pick out
any kind you like—flying,
walking, or swimming."

Grace chose a pterodactyl.

She copied it perfectly

from the encyclopedia.

It was fabulous.

Claude's apatosaurus was

wonderful.

Yoko finished her stegosaurus
early and helped one of the Frank
twins with his painting of
a flying raptor.

Everybody chose a wonderful
dinosaur.

"Doris, how about yours?" asked
Mrs. Jenkins.

"I can't," said Doris.

"Let me help," offered Grace.

"I don't want help," said Doris.

Doris dipped her paintbrush into the blue color.

She swirled it on the paper.

Then Doris dipped her blue brush in the yellow paint.

It turned green.

She painted green blobs.

After that, Doris put down her
brush in disgust.

"See!" said Doris with a snort.

"I can't paint!"

Everyone noticed Doris's painting,
but no one said anything about it.

Mrs. Jenkins hung all the pictures

in the hallway of Hilltop School.

Everyone admired them.

But Doris knew everyone hated

her painting.

"Doris," said Mrs. Jenkins, "you

don't have to paint anything

you don't want to."

But Doris knew everyone laughed
at her because she could not paint
a dinosaur. If Doris found someone
looking too hard at her blue swirl,
she thwacked her tail loudly on the
floor to scare them away.

One day during playtime,

Doris came inside for

a drink of water. Charles was

staring at Doris's blue swirl.

He was smiling.

"What are you looking at?"

asked Doris.

"I am looking at your painting,"

said Charles.

"Why? Why are you looking?"

asked Doris.

"I like it," said Charles.

"I don't believe you!" said Doris.

"No, really, I like it," said Charles.

"This picture makes me feel

all peaceful inside."

"You're crazy!" said Doris.

But every day before rest time,
Charles stood in the hall and
looked at Doris's picture.
Charles sighed, and then
closed his eyes.

"Charles seems to like your
picture, Doris," said Mrs. Jenkins.
"He's crazy," said Doris.

"Oh, I don't think so,"

said Mrs. Jenkins.

"Now, what are we doing

tomorrow, class?"

"We are going to the museum to

see the dinosaurs!" said everyone.

"That's right," said Mrs. Jenkins.

"Remember to bring your

dinosaur notebooks, one dollar

spending money, and your lunch."

Mr. Ossio showed everybody

around the museum.

In the first room were the bones

of a very old woolly mammoth.

"Is a woolly mammoth a dinosaur,

boys and girls?" asked Mr. Ossio.

"No!" answered everyone.

"Why not?" asked Mr. Ossio.

"Because a woolly mammoth

is a mammal!" answered

almost everyone.

"What a smart class with

a good teacher!" said Mr. Ossio.

"Take out your notebooks, class,"

said Mrs. Jenkins.

Timothy drew a hundred-toothed

rattlesnake.

Yoko drew a pincher turtle.

"What's your picture, Doris?"

asked Grace.

"I can't draw," said Doris.

"Let me show you how,"

said Grace.

Grace showed Doris how to draw

a woolly mammoth.

After Grace left,

Doris colored her whole page

with her red marker.

Then she put little black dots

in the middle.

Yoko looked at it.

She said nothing.

"You think I am stupid,"

said Doris.

Soon it was time for lunch.

Lunch was in the garden.

Mrs. Jenkins began to count heads.

She could not find Charles.

"Charles, where are you?"

Mrs. Jenkins called.

Charles did not come.

"Everyone!" said Mrs. Jenkins.

"Please put down your sandwiches
and find Charles."

Claude found him.

"Where were you?"

asked Mrs. Jenkins.

"I was in the other part of the

museum," said Charles.

"Come see!"

Everyone ate their sandwiches

and followed Charles.

Mr. Ossio was the guide.

"Oooh!" said everyone.

"What are these?" asked Grace.

"These are paintings by

one of the most wonderful artists

in the world," said Mr. Ossio.

"The artist's name was

Henri Matisse."

Everybody stared.

There on the far wall

was a blue swirl.

On the right wall was a red square

with little black dots.

"What do you think about these

pictures, boys and girls?"

asked Mr. Ossio.

For a long, long time

nobody answered.

Then Doris's hand went up.

"What do you think, young lady?"

asked Mr. Ossio.

"I guess Mr. Matisse didn't feel like drawing dinosaurs," said Doris.

On the bus ride home, everyone noticed that Doris was smiling the whole way.

31

Dear Parents,

When our children were young we lived in a small house, but we always made a space just for books. When their dad or I would read a story out loud, the TV was always off—radio and music, too—because it intruded.

Soon this peaceful half hour of every day became like a little island vacation. Our children are lifetime readers now with an endless curiosity for the rich world waiting between the covers of good books. It cost us nothing but time well spent and a library card.

This set of easy-to-read books is about the real nitty-gritty of elementary school. There are new friends, and bullies, too. There are germs and the "Clean Hands" song, new ways of painting pictures, learning music, telling the truth, gossiping, teasing, laughing, crying, separating from Mama, scary Halloweens, and secret valentines. The stories are all drawn from the experiences my children had in school.

It's my hope that these books will transport you and your children to a setting that's familiar, yet new, a place where you can explore the exciting new world of school together.

Rosemary Wells